D1221944

CN
CARTOON NETWORK
ADVENTURE TIME
VOLUME 1
BMO

ROSS RICHIE CEO & Founder • **JOY HUFFMAN** CFO • **MATT GAGNON** Editor-in-Chief • **FILIP SABLIK** President, Publishing & Marketing • **STEPHEN CHRISTY** President, Development • **LANCE KREITER** Vice President, Licensing & Merchandising
PHIL BARBARO Vice President, Finance & Human Resources • **ARUNE SINGH** Vice President, Marketing • **BRYCE CARLSON** Vice President, Editorial & Creative Strategy • **SCOTT NEWMAN** Manager, Production Design • **KATE HENNING** Manager, Operations
SPENCER SIMPSON Manager, Sales • **SIERRA HAHN** Executive Editor • **JEANINE SCHAEFER** Executive Editor • **DAFNA PLEBAN** Senior Editor • **SHANNON WATTERS** Senior Editor • **ERIC HARBURN** Senior Editor
WHITNEY LEOPARD Editor • **CAMERON CHITTOCK** Editor • **CHRIS ROSA** Editor • **MATTHEW LEVINE** Editor • **SOPHIE PHILIPS-ROBERTS** Assistant Editor • **GAVIN GRONENTHAL** Assistant Editor • **MICHAEL MOCCIO** Assistant Editor
AMANDA LaFRANCO Executive Assistant • **JILLIAN CRAB** Design Coordinator • **MICHELLE ANKLEY** Design Coordinator • **KARA LEOPARD** Production Designer • **MARIE KRUPINA** Production Designer • **GRACE PARK** Production Design Assistant
CHELSEA ROBERTS Production Design Assistant • **ELIZABETH LOUGHRIDGE** Accounting Coordinator • **STEPHANIE HOCUTT** Social Media Coordinator • **JOSÉ MEZA** Event Coordinator • **HOLLY AITCHISON** Operations Coordinator
MEGAN CHRISTOPHER Operations Assistant • **RODRIGO HERNANDEZ** Mailroom Assistant • **MORGAN PERRY** Direct Market Representative • **CAT O'GRADY** Marketing Assistant • **BREANNA SARPY** Executive Assistant

ADVENTURE TIME Volume One, December 2018. Published by KaBOOM!, a division of Boom Entertainment, Inc. ADVENTURE TIME, CARTOON NETWORK, the logos, and all related characters and elements are trademarks of and © Cartoon Network. (S18) Originally published in single magazine form as ADVENTURE TIME No. 1-4, ADVENTURE TIME FREE COMIC BOOK DAY EDITION. © Cartoon Network. (S12) All rights reserved. KaBOOM!™ and the KaBOOM! logo are trademarks of Boom Entertainment, Inc., registered in various countries and categories. All characters, events, and institutions depicted herein are fictional. Any similarity between any of the names, characters, persons, events, and/or institutions in this publication to actual names, characters, and persons, whether living or dead, events, and/or institutions is unintended and purely coincidental. KaBOOM! does not read or accept unsolicited submissions of ideas, stories, or artwork.

BOOM! Studios, 5670 Wilshire Boulevard, Suite 400, Los Angeles, CA 90036-5679. Printed in China. Eighth Printing.

ISBN: 978-1-60886-280-1, eISBN: 978-1-61398-031-6

CREATED BY
Pendleton Ward

WRITTEN BY
Ryan North

ILLUSTRATED BY
Shelli Paroline and Braden Lamb

"BMO'S LESSON"
ILLUSTRATED BY
Mike Holmes
COLORS BY STUDIO PARLAPÁ

LETTERS BY
Steve Wands

COVER BY
Chris Houghton
COLORS BY KASSANDRA HELLER

EDITOR
Shannon Watters

ASSISTANT EDITOR
Adam Staffaroni

TRADE DESIGN & "BMO IN THE DESERT" ILLUSTRATIONS BY
Stephanie Gonzaga

"BMO IN THE DESERT" COLORS BY
KASSANDRA HELLER

With special thanks to
Marisa Marionakis, Rick Blanco, Curtis Lelash, Laurie Halal-Ono, Keith Mack, Kelly Crews and the wonderful folks at Cartoon Network.

Okay dude!
Three...two...
one...
BUMP!
Awesome!
What are we
gonna do with the
footage?
Aw, I'm
sure we'll find
a use for it
somewhere.

ADVENTURE TIME
Jake the Dog: Magical dog with stretchy powers. Pal rating at 110%!
Finn the Human: Awesome dude with awesome hat. Pal rating at 110%!
The Land of Ooo: A pretty magical place! Jake and Finn live here. Adventure possibility: UNLIMITED??
Really good at being pals AND at adventures!
The Lich: HE IS COMING.
Ice King: All he wants to do is marry a princess, and he thinks stealing them is okay!
Marceline th
Vampire Queen
Over a thousan
years old. Be cool, okay?
Princess Bubblegum: Human/bubblegum ruler of the Candy Kingdom. She's made of gum! She and Finn are friends, and sometimes feelings can get complicated, you know?
Not as important as the other boxes, just a heads up.
Written by Ryan North
Art by Shelli Paroline and Braden Lamb
"Adventure Time" created by Pendleton Ward
BMO runs on electricity and likes taking nice pictures!
Not pictured is the EARL OF LEMONGRAB, who is currently sitting in a chair in an empty room, screaming.

Uh oh.

There's another sign just out of frame that says, "Look at this workmanship and I'm sure you'll see / Ain't nobody better at making quick, extremely accurate signs than

OH DANG! WE'LL GET BACK TO THE LICH,
BUT FIRST IN ANOTHER PART OF OOO...

BMO'S LESSON!

WITH

JAKE

"THE DOG"

FINN

"THE HUMAN"

BUBBLEGUM

"THE PRINCESS"

BMO

"THE COMPUTER"

FOUR DAYS LATER...
I want to be the best BMO I can be, Princess! I want to be the best BMO.
You are the best BMO!

No, because sometimes, I have made little mistakes.
Aw, we all make mistakes!
BMO

PFFFT
BMO

See? I make mistakes too: I grabbed the wrong milk. This isn't from cows!
You... drink from cows?

Yeah, sometimes.
But I am a computer, Princess! I was programmed to be perfect.
...I think?

Well, what do you want to be perfect at?
I WANT TO BE PERFECT AT FIGHTS!!

But I don't even know how to start them. How do you know when it's time for fights, Princess?
Come on, you don't want to start fights!
I want to punch bad guys!!
BMO

BAD GUY! Take punch 1!
And here's punch 2!
I HAVE PUNCHES 3 THROUGH 65,535 ALREADY PREPARED, BAD GUY!!
BMO

But I would never punch you, Princess.
Aw, BMO. I'd never punch you either.

Well, if you really want to get good at fights, you should **TRAIN!**
I should... train?

Choo choo!
BMO

SOON:
Thanks for joining us, Finn and Jake!
Not a problem! We're always ready to help out.
We're easy to the peasy!

Okay. I think we should star training wit punches.
Hi-yah!

Not bad! But you also need to know how to block a punch thrown at you. Boys?
Jake, I'm going to punch you but it's just for pretend!
Finn, I'm going to block your punch but it doesn't mean we're not still **ULTIMATE SUPER-BROS!**

Here come a bunch of good reasons and one smaller but still good reason why you're gonna get hurt!!
He's referring to his fingers and thumb!

Whoah! Jake! **NICE!**
Thanks! But watch out, buddy, because that compliment is going straight to my...

...HEAD!

Ha ha ha!
WHUMPH
CRUNCH

That was awesome, dude.
Heh. I thought you might like it!
But Jake, I can't do crazy messed up things with my head like that!

That's true. Jake, can you fight without your powers?
I dunno. Probably?
No powers! No powers!

Okay Finn, punch me again! I won't use my powers when I block it, honest.
Here it comes!

PUNCH
OW OW OW OW OW OW OW!

Fighting without powers is dumb and I hate it! People actually fight like that?
I do it ALL THE TIME!

YOU don't have any powers?
Nope! I'm just a guy. Come on buddy, you knew that.
SERIOUSLY?!
I fight without powers too.

Here, watch this, BMO. Finn, you punch me and I'll block it.
You promise?
Yes, come on. Give me your best shot.

Hooray!
KAPOW

That!
Was!
AWESOME!
My turn! My turn!

You sure? You only saw it once, that might not be enough to learn everything there is about flipping du--
I am a COMPUTER, Finn!

Okay, okay! Here comes the punch, BMO!

rrrrr...

Am I the best at fighting yet??

Maybe physical fighting isn't your thing, BMO! There are other ways you can fight: passive-aggressively, intellectually, with words, or--
Words! BMO can fight with words!!

BMO can fight with BATTLE BURNS.

What are battle burns?
I will teach you! Try to punch me!
Okay!

Battle burns are when you're punching me and I say...
ahem

CENSORED DUE TO BMO'S BATTLE BURN BEING SO GOOD, IT CAN'T LEGALLY BE RELEASED TO THE GENERAL PUBLIC!!

BMO, THAT WAS AMAZING!
Nice!
My mind, she is blown!

Can you teach us... battle burns??
I'd love to use them at the royal court!!

OON:
To do a battle burn, you need to think of the punches you'd like to punch, and then turn them all into words instead!
You mean up in my brain? I mean, up in my skull walnut?
Correct, Finn!

Hmm...
No punching...

Your sense of style is disagreeable to my aesthetic tastes.

This is hard, BMO!

Is it like when I'm punching someone's head off so it flies up into the sky, and I say something like "Heads up"? Or "Here, I'll give you a HEAD START"?
No! No Finn, that's not a burn at all! Those are puns, that's totally different!

I can see this is going to take a lot of work.

Okay, imagine that YOUR feelings...are actually the feelings of the person you are fighting!
That's just crazy enough to work!!
And now, try to hurt those feelings!
Jake, I think if you applied yourself harder you could accomplish some really amazing things.
Thank you dude; I believe the same.
No, no, no! Princess, can you help them?
Finn! Jake! When I look at you, my eyes show me some reasonable-looking dudes...
...because they know that the slightest comprehension of your actual faces would be to gaze into THE UNBLINKING EYE OF MADNESS!!
Hooray! Princess you have graduated from Level 1 of my class!
Nothing personal, guys.
I've got to get back to Official Princess Business, but this has been a lot of fun. I'll keep practicing!
Bye Princess! Thank you for the cookies!
Why can't you both be more like my star pupil?
I think she's just naturally good at battle burns!
I think she's just naturally good at not being bad at things.

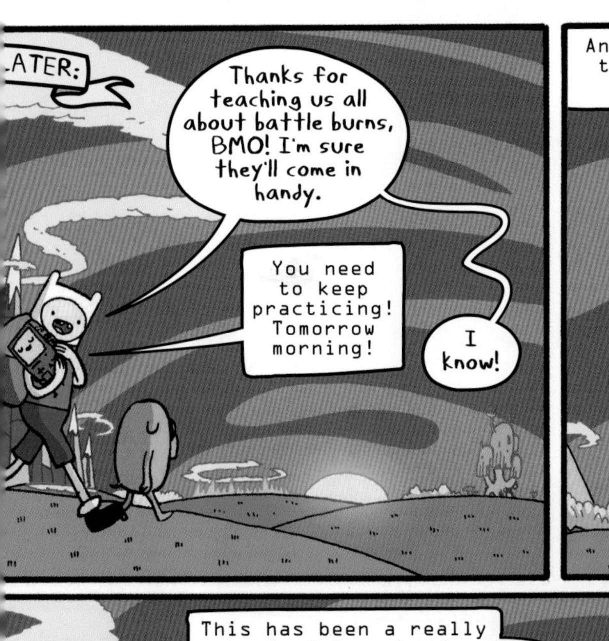

This has been a really wonderful weekend.

It has, hasn't it? I don't think anything could happen now to ruin it.

It is not possible for **ANYTHING** and/or **ANYONE** to ruin this weekend, dude!

Okay dude, try this one on for size!
"Your mom called...!"

"She said it was time to o home and stop bothering us. She said she has to talk to you **THROUGH US** because she's so ashamed."
Sweet!!
But scope this:

"You call **THAT** a 'punch'? Because it seems more just like **WATERED-DOWN FRUIT JUICE!** It's disappointing, and makes me sad."

Huh. I don't think that was a very good battle burn.
Hey man, I appreciate your honesty.

KRAKA-DOOM

Was that **YOU?**

Uncool, Lich.
You know what we gotta do, buddy...

Found them!
Asymptotic!
Slant asymptotic, dude!

I knew it was cool for a dude to keep anti-mind-control jewelry around the house.
Man, you know I don't judge. I kinda like wearing jewelry too sometimes.
We can talk about that later...

Man, there sure are some cool things buried in the dirt. I refer both to this comic book page **AND** to real life in general.

FOOLS. I WILL SUCK EVERYTHING YOU'VE EVER KNOWN INTO THIS BAG AND THEN I WILL THROW IT INTO THE SUN. DO YOU REALLY THINK A BOY AND HIS BLOBBY DOG CAN STOP ME?

Yeah, we do!

THEN WATCH. WATCH AS YOUR PLANET DIES.
NEVER!

This is serious, dude. This is a real end-of-the-world scenario. I think we both know what we have to...nay, GET to do.
I hear you, man. Let's DO THIS!

Ready?
Ready!

ere can never be enough fist bumps in any story, whether fiction or non-fiction. DID YOU KNOW: This is one of the few universally-accepted rules of literature?

I DON'T THINK I WILL.

LOOK:
YOU'RE WASTING YOUR TIME.

PRINCESS BUBBLEGUM!

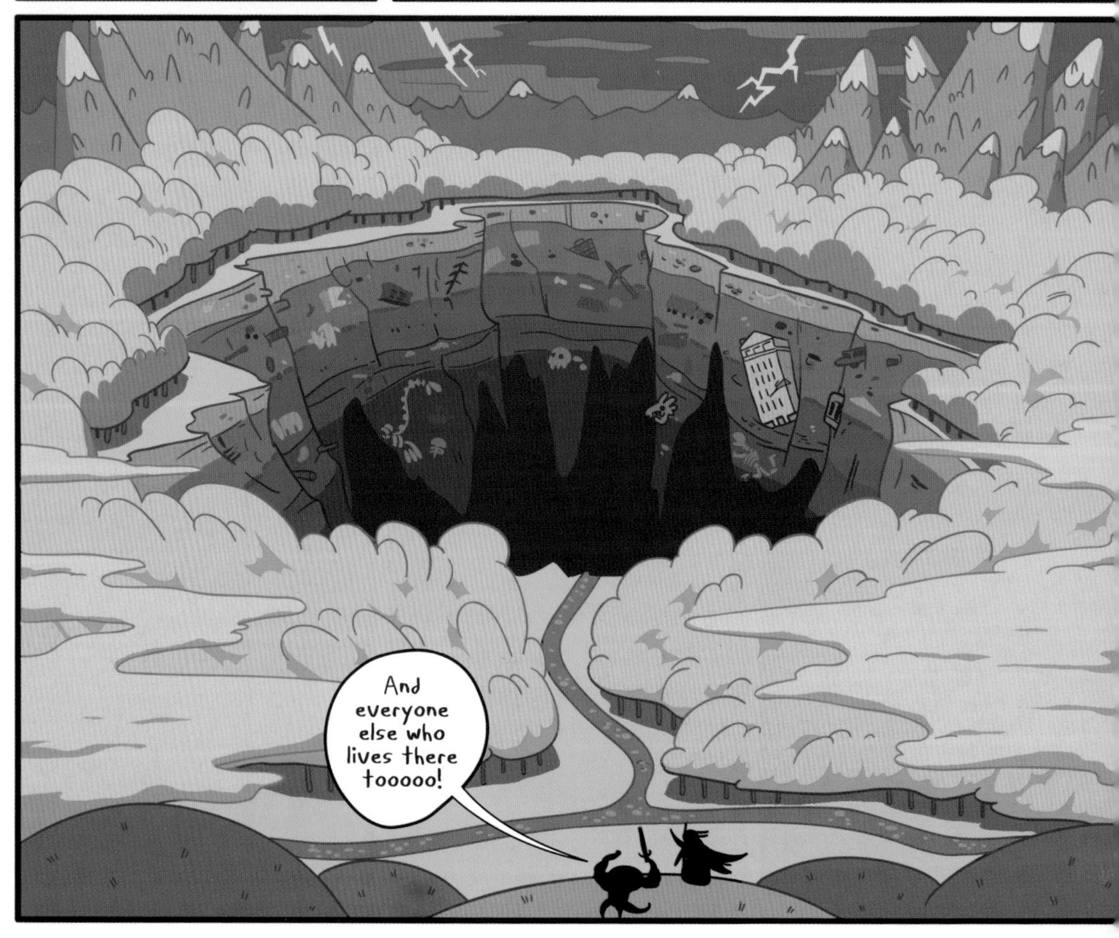
And everyone else who lives there tooooo!

AND NOW, YOU.
NO!
NOOOOOOOOOO!
NNOOOOOOOOOOOOOOOOOOOOOOOOOOOOOOOOOOOOOOOOOOOOO!
I don't think he can hear us in here, dude.

Where are we?! Where's the way out? The Lich's butt isn't going to kick itself!
WE NEED TO HELP IT DO THAT, JAKE!!

Huh.
Maybe she knows?

Gentlemen! Hello!

Hello, your highness! I'm Jake the Dog, and this is my friend, Finn the Human. We're going to stop The Lich! He's uh, a skeleton dude. I think? It's gross. I dunno.
He's a gross jerk!!

I think we may have something in common, gentlemen, for it was THAT VERY SAME GROSS JERK who sent me here! Greetings Finn and Jake, and welcome to my kingdom.
I'm Desert Princess.

And it is very nice to meet you!!
SHAKE
SHAKE
SHAKE
SHAKE
SHAKE
SHAKE

- We must've stayed together on our way into the bag because we were in Jake Suit mode!

I love Jake Suit, dude. -

MEANWHILE, IN THE ICE KINGDOM:
Hmm... Yes, that's DEFINITELY what she'd say.
write
write
write
write
Whaaa--?!
Gunter!
My fan fiction!!
FIONNA & CAKE MEET FINN & JAKE

THOSE ARE MY TWO PERSONAL PROJECTS!!

Wait... you again?

SAND
QUEST
3
BMO

BMO

THE LAND OF Ooo:
YES.
EVERYTHING IS GOING PERFECTLY.

If this were an audio comic you could hear what Marceline was playing and, faced with hearing such beauty, your ears would weep.

Desert Princess is as mysterious as she is...made out of desserts.

But I still think we need to escape this bag, Jake.
AW MAN!

How come we ALWAYS have to save the world JUST as I finish up the best castle eve--

--nevermind let's go.

Well. Maybe we should search that-a-way?
ON IT, Princess. WHAT TIME IS IT??

ADDDDVENTURE TIME!!
Time to escape this bag!!

Oh, I didn't know you two had your own thing going.
Sorry.

What time is it??

AD VENTURE TIME!

FINN AND JAKE'S ADVERTISING CORPORATION

If we just pick a direction and run, we're bound to hit the edge of the bag eventually!!
SCIENCE.
Yes!

TWENTY MINUTES LATER:
Man, I'm pooped. I don't think running is the answer here, dudes. I think running--I think running might actually be the worst.

Gentlemen! Maybe we're thinking too two-dimensionally! Maybe we can escape...up?

Anything's better than runnninnngggg
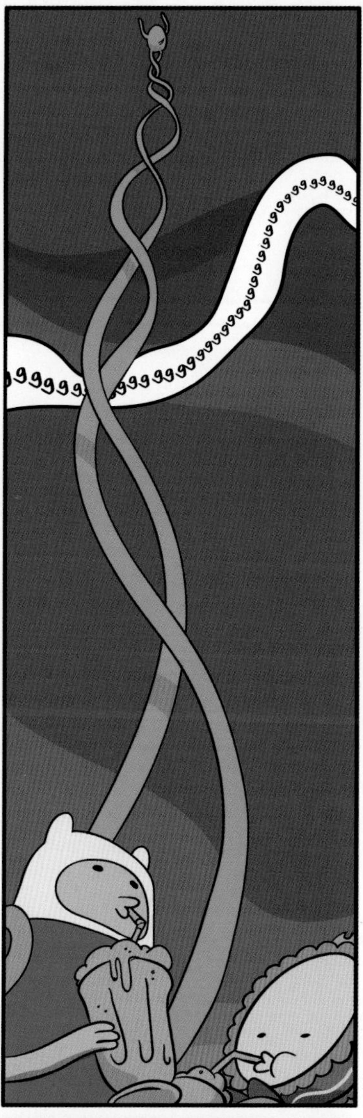
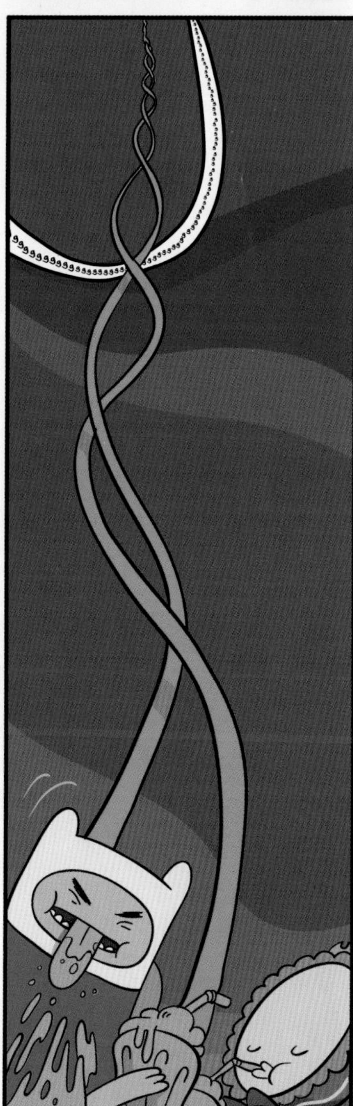

Remember when the Lich was attacking me and my totally sweet house?
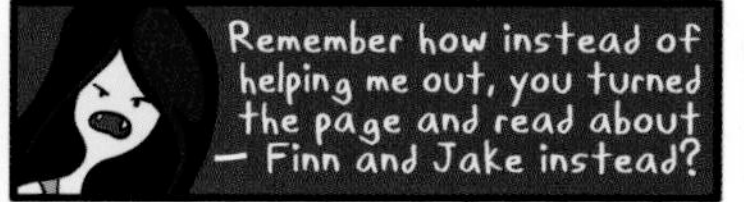
Remember how instead of helping me out, you turned the page and read about Finn and Jake instead?

Well I don't have to remember because he's still attacking me and IT'S HAPPENING RIGHT NOW!!

MEANWHILE:
You're SUCH a JERK!!
HA HA HA!

You're asking for it, little man.
I'M ASKING FOR IT.

ENOUGH!!
NO.

NO, IT'S NEVER ENOUGH.

What? You didn't help me out AGAIN?!

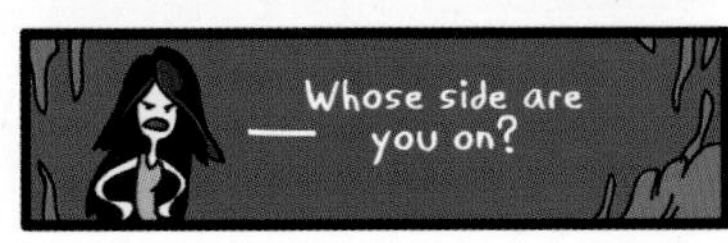
Whose side are you on?

Because you could've been on TEAM VAMPIRE QUEEN.

As soon as I get out of here, SOMEONE's gonna get their butt kicked!
Obvs!

Who's there?! Hynden, is that you?

No, Marceline, it's me.

Wow. Way to dress, Bonnibel.
Royal dresses are too warm for the beach! Don't be mean!

So, you know a way off this island?
Maybe. What else can you turn into, besides bats and wolves and monsters?

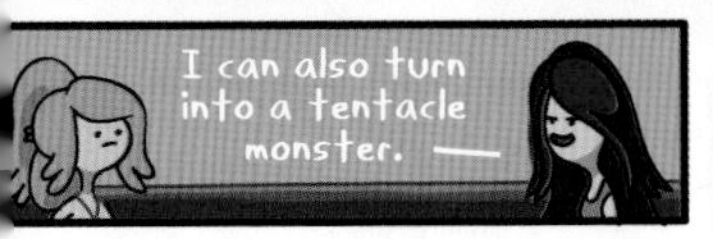

I can also turn into a tentacle monster.

HOW DOES THAT HELP OUR SITUATION?

HOW DOES IT HURT OUR SITUATION, THOUGH?

"Greetings, Jake!!" said cake, stretching herself to form the words "Greetings, Jake!!"

Is this some sort of...metaphorical language relying on an ancient cultural misunderstanding of the heart being the center of emotion??

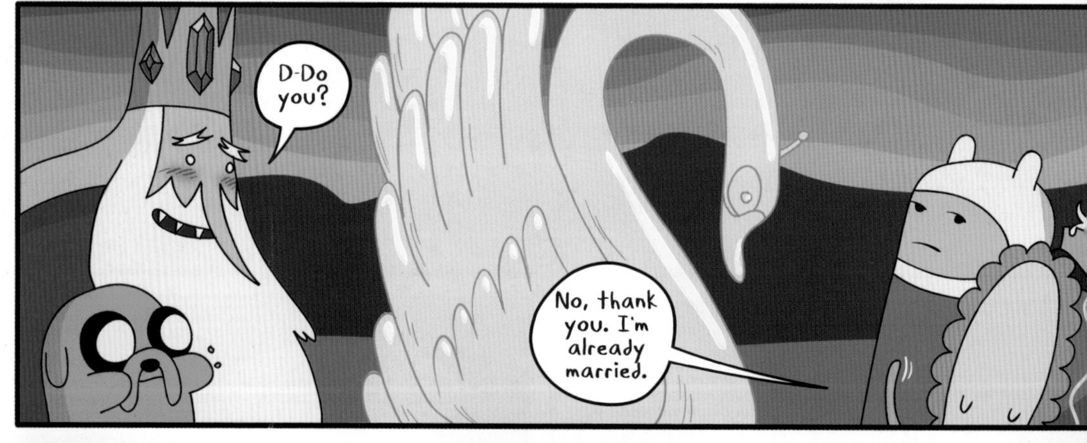

I'VE BEEN DOING IT SINCE LIKE FOREVER

Let's learn more about the Earth's crust! As you may have heard, yes, it is mainly made out of old crusts.

Melissa? MELISSA! Skeleton guy made me say all that junk!

Zero bars?! I hate this lumping phone!
SPLAT

Hey there, guys.
Ugh.
Dudes, we're not making any progress on saving the world here!! In fact, we're making NEGATIVE progress, because now Lumpy Space Princess is here and all we've done is HAVE A PICNIC!

I made the ice!
Though it was very nice of you to make it for us, Desert Princess.
Thank you.

What do you want us to do, man? We've looked on the ground AND in the sky! There's nowhere else to look, unless somehow we could tunnel through the ground itself with some sort of amazing d--

AMAZING DRILL HANDS!!

To be fair, it's extremely hard NOT to hate a lumping phone with zero bars.

BUMP

How come the tunnel is lit when there's no torches? It's the same way the inside of the bag is lit when there's no sun: SCIENCE. Wait no hold on wait wait I meant to say MAGIC.

Okay. Ready, Jake?
Ready, Finn.
WHAT TIME IS IT??

ADVENTURE TIME!!

WHOA!!
THIS WASN'T PART OF THE PLAN!!!
SCHLORRP

ELSEWHERE:
Land ho!

Your watch may say it's 3:44 pm but that's just code for ADVENTURE TIME.

Where?
Over there! But we're not gonna get there if you're not the sail.

Fine, jeez. Bossy much?
Marcy, I'm the SKIPPER.

SOON:
I could use some help!
SORRY! TOO BUSY BEING THE SAIL HERE, SKIP!

What do you think Finn and Jake are up to?
Aw, they're probably beating bad guys up as we speak. I'm sure we've got nothing to worry about.

What the cabbage?
PRINCESS BUBBLEGUM! PRINCESS BUBBLEGUM!! OH MY GLOB IT'S TERRIBLE! IT'S SO SAD!
Ladies, I don't really know how to say this, but...well--

FINN AND JAKE ARE TOTALLY DEAD!!

HA HA HA YES!

Wow. I am
pretty bored in
I gotta

BMO

ARTH (WHAT'S LEFT OF IT, ANYWAY):

HA HA HA!

AND THAT'S HOW THE LICH WON AND THE EARTH WAS DESTROYED FOREVER.

Thank you for going on this journey with us! This is...

The End

was
Written by Ryan North
Art was done by Shelli Paroline and Braden Lamb
was Lettered by Steve Wands
"Adventure Time" created by Pendleton Ward

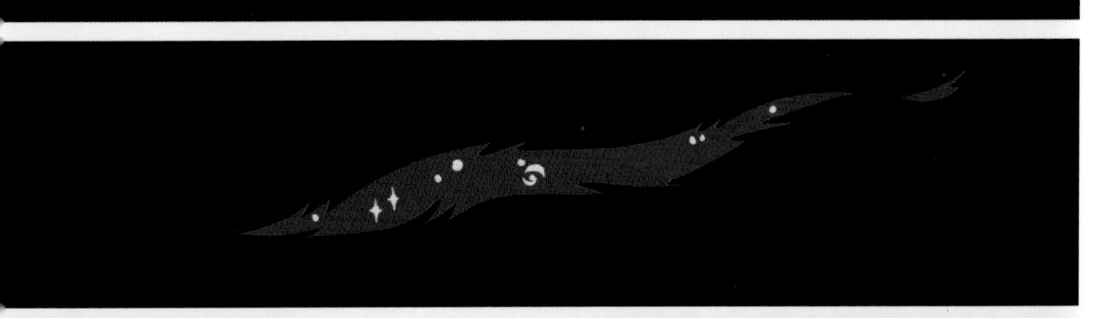

I was going to make this and all the remaining pages in the book entirely black and have the last page say "Hey, didn't you read the page sixty. It's over!" but then Jake and Finn burst out of the bag. They saved both the day *AND* the quality of this comic!

Those gemstones Finn and Jake are wearing also allow them to magically breathe and talk in space! This feature wasn't mentioned before because there's always been lots of air around, so it just never came up. You might even be wearing clothes that allow you to magically breathe and talk in space right now! *HOW WOULD YOU KNOW?*

ternate, worse line for Princess Bubblegum: "That's okay, it's PLANE what's going on!" (because of Jet Jake) (did you know: not all puns are good?!)

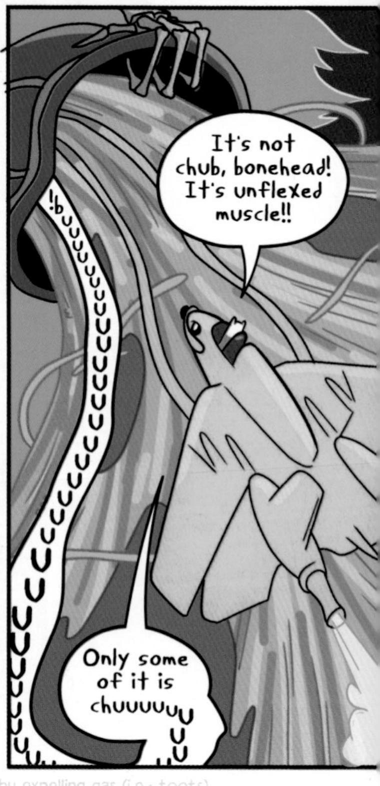

Jet Jake moves in space the same way spaceships move in space: by expelling gas (i.e.: toots)

Jake slide, Jake slide / His body gets longer than it is wide

Some people say they prefer working alone to working in groups, but I bet that's just because they've never had Finn propose a team to them before!

AWESOME:
It's been a sl-ICE!
Man, that didn't make sense. You're not even attacking with a sword!

Oh wait, I get itttttttttttttttttttttttt

You want some science in your face??

It appears he didn't want science in OR about his face, Princess.

Hey Lich! Looks like you've got to TAKE YOUR LUMPS!
Oh my glob that's SO racist.

OW! He's just skin and bones and I lumpin' bit myself!!
Like I need more lumpin' LUMPS!

My crown protects me from the Lich's mind control!
Mine too!

High five?
If I high five you, will you try to kidnap me?

Ye--um, I mean, uh...there's one way to find out?

Everyone's landing in the same place because now they have the power of *TEAMS* to keep them together. Teamwork is the real power!
It's about 1.5 joules per second; ask any scientist!

Lumpy Space Princess is secretly really happy here because she got the task of spreading gossip around to a bunch of people. That's *BASICALLY* her dream job!

SOON:
This is really appealing to me for some reason.
I know what you mean, dude.
And then he calls me "talky," and it's like, YEAH, at least I've got something worth saying!!

Looks like we're ready here, Finn.
Alright. Put your gem on, Jake.
Oh, it's ON.

Ha, I didn't even mean that in the "let's go fight" sense! It totally works though.
Heh. Crazy.

I've ordered the first wave of Elemental Finns and Jakes to follow you in, Finn!
Perfect! We're going in!!

Marceline! Remember you promised to give me back my crown in one piece!

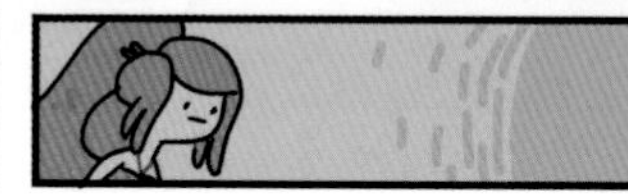

Don't get hurt.

NOW, MARCELINE!

Look at this guy, he's the big stupid Lich!
We keep popping out his bag, 'cause he never learned to STITCH!

Wants to kill all life, well at least he found his niche!
Before he goes ahead with that he'd better hear our PITCH!

If I'd summed him up with one word, I probably go with "jerk"!
Our battle rap's so super tight, it's driving him BERZERK!

It's almost like she aimed me here, wow, isn't that strange?
What sort of crazy thing could we be trying to ARRANGE?

NOW, Jake!!
On it!

Good luck or whatever, Finn. I mean it. I'm being serious.
And good luck, Mr. Jake.
And good luck, M--
And Ice King? Good luck to Ice King? Hello?
See ya Princesses!

You suck me in your bag, man, you know I'm coming back!
If I were you right now I'd have anxiety ATTACKS!

You dumb to do something again, expectin' different things to happen!
The only thing that changed is that we all just started RAPPIN'!

We're gonna end this soon, Lich.
So don't you even blink!
We're gonna see what happens when I...

NO!
NO!!
...start to...

...SHRINK!
RIIIP

PWOOSH

WHOA!

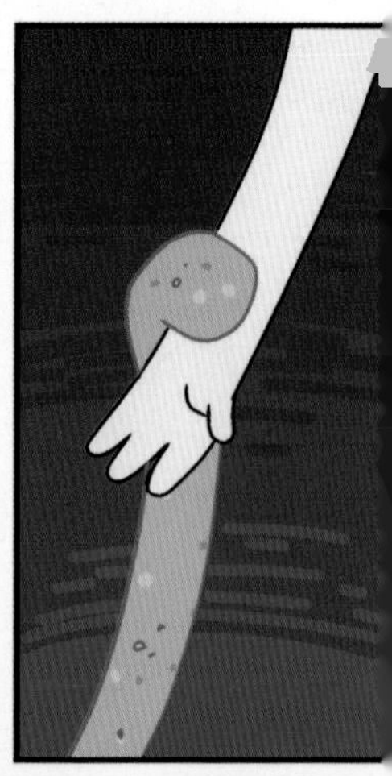

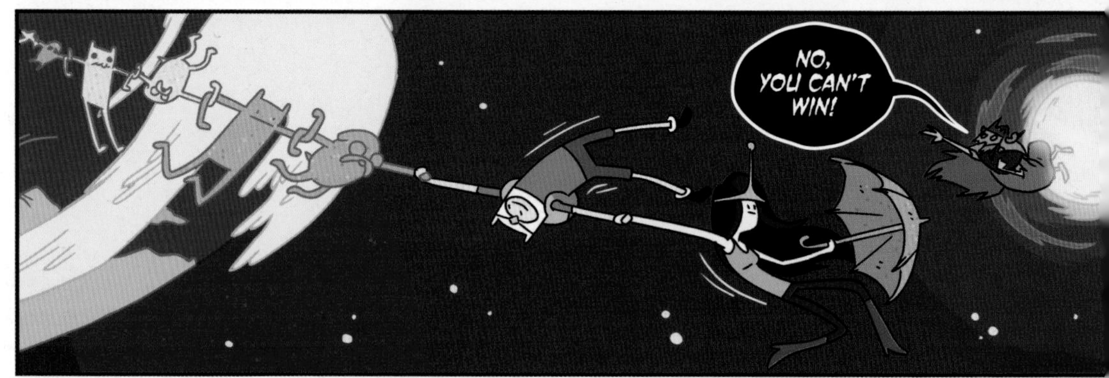
NO, YOU CAN'T WIN!

NNNOOOOOOoooo!

We did it! We won!!
And our spontaneous RHYMING battle burns? AMAZING.

Wait...no, wait, Finn--something's not right.
The Land of Ooo is... MISSING?

How do you avoid saying "woosh!" 24/7, Marceline?

BEHIND THE SCENES FACT: All of Adventure Time, the show *AND* the comic, was leading up to Finn's pun in panel three. *ALL OF IT.*

Dear Breakfast Kingdom: I would live in you. I would take all my meals in you, including lunch and dinner. *I'M EVEN INCLUDING DESSERT.* I'm not messing around here. Breakfast Kingdom.

Butts to the both of you! Good day!!

PRO TIP: if you want to grow up to marry a princess, do exactly the opposite of whatever Ice King does! You'll be off to a *TERRIFIC* start.

I thought it was just a new form of ice: "crunchy ice that tastes bad in my drinks and also fails to cool them"?

I just assumed I was seeing things! The sand goes on forever, Finn. There's got to be enough there to...
...to fill in a giant hole?!
...I was gonna say "feed an army" but sure.

WAIT, THAT'S IT! All we have to do is take all the sand covering the world and stick it in that giant hole!
Yes, Jake?

How are we gonna do that, dude? The planet is huge and there's sand everywhere!
I have an idea, Mr. Finn!

What if I used some sand to make a sand version of...myself? Then Sand Me could make another Sand Me, and so on!
Then they all just walk into the hole and jump in!

I've never done a sand version of myself before, but it should work. Right?

Psammo!
Psammo!
Psammo!
Psammo!
Psammo!
Psammo!
Psammo!
Psammo!

SOON:
Okay, this area's clean now, and there's a wave of me making more me spreading across the surface of the planet. That'll take care of the sand, Mister Finn!
Perfect!

ATTENTION, DESERT PRINCESSES!
Wait, hold on a second.

Should it be "Desert Princesses" or "Deserts Princess"?
I dunno, man. I think it's the first one.
Nice. Thanks.

ATTENTION, DESERT PRINCESSES! WALK EAST UNTIL YOU FIND A GIANT HOLE, OKAY? THEN JUMP IN AND FILL IT UP WITH SAND, OKAY? SOUND GOOD?
WHAT IF WE DON'T WANT TO DO THAT THOUGH?

Hello, I'm Desert Princess!

Hah, we're both saying the same thing at the same time!

I like your name!!

WHAT IF--AND THIS IS EMBARRASSING BUT, WELL, WHAT IF WE ALL HAVE A BIT OF A CRUSH ON YOU, FINN?
You guys!! Don't say that!
BUT IT'S TRUE.

AND WE DON'T WANT TO DISAPPEAR WITHOUT GETTING ONE LITTLE FINN KISS.
Oh my gosh oh my gosh this is so embarrassing!

But I can't kiss all of you! There's way too many. I'll get all puckered out!
NOT A PROBLEM, MISTER FINN.

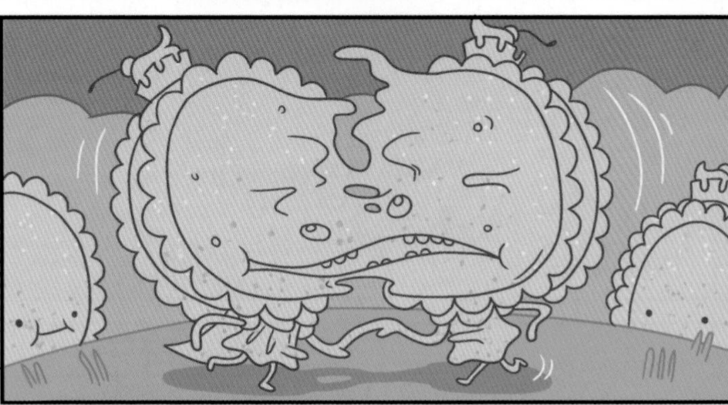

Welp, I'm out. That's my limit of crazy for today!
Um... ha ha

Suddenly everyone says "Hey, does it seem like the Earth's gravitational pull has increased on you too?"

Thanks for reading!

ONE THOUSAND YEARS AGO:
Whoa, check this place out!! And it even comes with a cool creepy bag! I could TOTALLY stay here until it's safe outside again.

Actually, I don't--I don't think I like this. It feels weird. It's kinda burning my hand.
Maybe I shouldn't be here after all.

Marcy, I know the mushroom bombs have...changed things. Awakened...things. And I know I've been alone for so long that I've started talking to myself.

But don't be afraid, Marceline! We're tough! We're smart!
We'll make it through this. I promise.

It's fine. There'll be somewhere else to stay. Somewhere else where we can find...friends. Besides, it can't stay like this forever, right?
...
Everything is gonna be fine.

It'll just take some time.

NOW:
the End
For Real This Time!
COMING SOON...
TIME-BENDING
ADVENTURES!!!

BM

COVER GALLERY

Cover 1A:
Shelli Paroline and Braden Lamb

Covers 1B & 1C:
Chris Houghton
Colors: Kassandra Heller

Cover 1D:
Jeffrey Brown

Emerald City Comicon Exclusive Cover:
Chris Samnee
Colors: Matthew Wilson

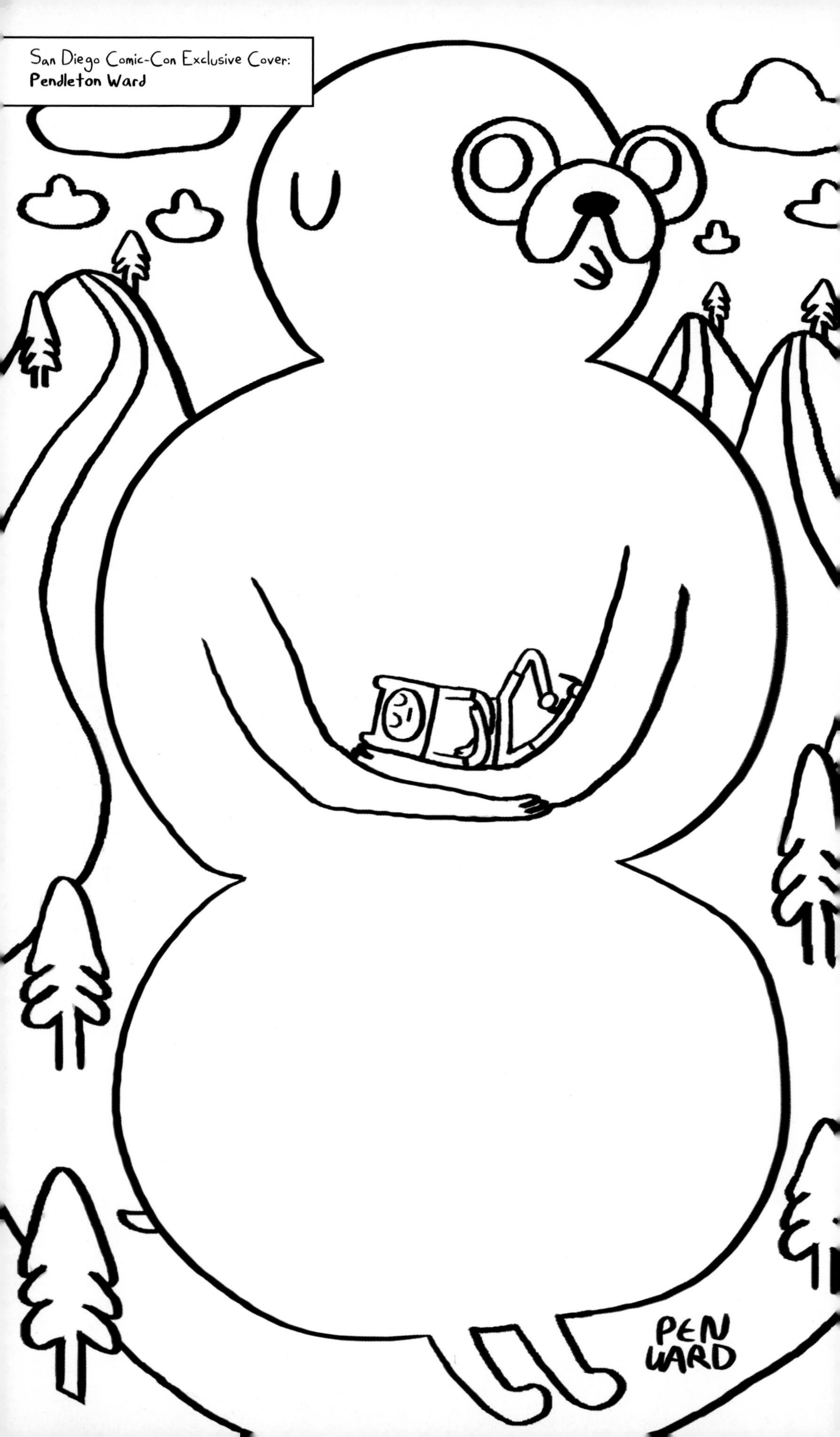
San Diego Comic-Con Exclusive Cover:
Pendleton Ward
PEN
WARD

Annapolis Comic-Con Exclusive Cover:
Sanford Greene

Issue #1 2nd Print:
Chris Houghton
Colors: Kassandra Heller

Issue #1 3rd Print:
Chris Houghton
Colors: Kassandra Heller
CHRIS HOUGHTON

Cover 2A:
Chris Houghton
Colors: Kassandra Heller
CHRIS HOUGHTON

Cover 2B:
JAB
Colors: Braden Lamb

Emily Carroll

Cover 2D:
Becky Dreistadt & Frank Gibson

Issue #2 2nd Print:
Chris Houghton
Colors: Kassandra Heller
CHRIS HOUGHTON

Cover 3A:
Chris Houghton
Colors: Kassandra Heller
CHRIS HOUGHTON

Cover 3B:
Elena Barbarich

Cover 3C:
Michael DeForge

Cover 3D:
Stephanie Buscema

Cover 4A:
Chris Houghton
Colors: Kassandra Heller

Cover 4B:
Kassandra Heller
Kassandra
HELLER

Cover 4C:
Scott C.
Scott C.

Cover 4D:
Bettie Ward

Maine Comic Arts Festival Exclusive:
Melanie Tingdahl
Colors: Lisa Moore
mt12

Double Midnight Comics Exclusive:
Mike Holmes
Colors: Lisa Moore

BM

FROM SCRIPT TO PAGE!

BY RYAN NORTH

Above you can see the final page as it appears in ADVENTURE TIME Volume 1 (page 43). I thought I'd show how the script compares to the final page!

In issue one, I wrote out page layouts for Braden and Shelli, saying things like "we've got these panels 1x3 on the page, and then a splashy panel 4, and then panel 5 long and skinny beneath that". But then they surprised me with rough pencils that A) used my layouts in a few cases but B) came up with way better ones a ton of the time. So in this issue (and onwards!) I just said "hey, here are the panels with what's happening inside of them" and let Braden and Shelli do the layouts. They're awesome at it!

PAGE FIVE

Panel 1:
Jake (big) with Finn on his back and DP being pulled up by Finn, as he runs off at full speed. Finn is helping DP up by her hands.
FINN: If we just pick a direction and run, we're bound to hit the edge of the bag eventually!!
DP: Yes!
JAKE: SCIENCE.

Panel 2:
NARRATION: Twenty minutes later:
Jake, flopped out on the ground, exhausted, legs splayed, Finn standing beside him, DP is on her knees in the sand building something.
JAKE: Man, I'm pooped. I don't think running is the answer here, dudes. I think running--I think running might actually be the worst.

Panel 3:
DP has made three sand drinks with straws. She offers the extras to Finn and Jake.
DP: Gentlemen! Maybe we're thinking too two-dimensionally! Maybe we can escape...up?

Panel 4:
We see a low-angle looking up with Finn and DP as Jake spirals off into the sky, legs still on the ground. Finn and DP staring upwards. Finn is taking the offered drink absent-mindedly.
JAKE (words getting smaller as he blasts into the sky): Anything's better than runninggggggg

Panel 5:
Same angle, but now Finn and DP sip on their sand drinks while they stare at Jake going up into the sky.

Panel 6:
Same angle, but now Finn tastes what he's drinking and spits out sand while DP continues to sip and stare upwards at Jake.

ALT: a little tiny comic at the bottom of the page featuring Marceline, addressing the camera.
P1: Remember when the Lich was attacking me and my totally sweet house?
P2: Remember how instead of helping me out, you turned the page and read about Finn and Jake instead?
p3: Well I don't have to remember because he's still attacking me and IT'S HAPPENING RIGHT NOW!!

For example, check out the long, tall panels they drew on this page! They work SO WELL and communicate the heights that Jake's reaching up to in a really nice visual way. But it's not just layout: in the script I have Jake's "Anything's better than runninggggggg" line happen in panel 4, but here in the comic his dialogue is spread out across panels 5 and 6 too, being pulled up with Jake as he stretches himself higher. Nice! It makes the page more fun to look at (and read!) and we get the sense of Jake's words fading away as he gets higher up, which is exactly what I was going for. It's always awesome when you can translate vocal effects like this to a silent, visual medium, and still have them come through like I'm whispering into your ear!

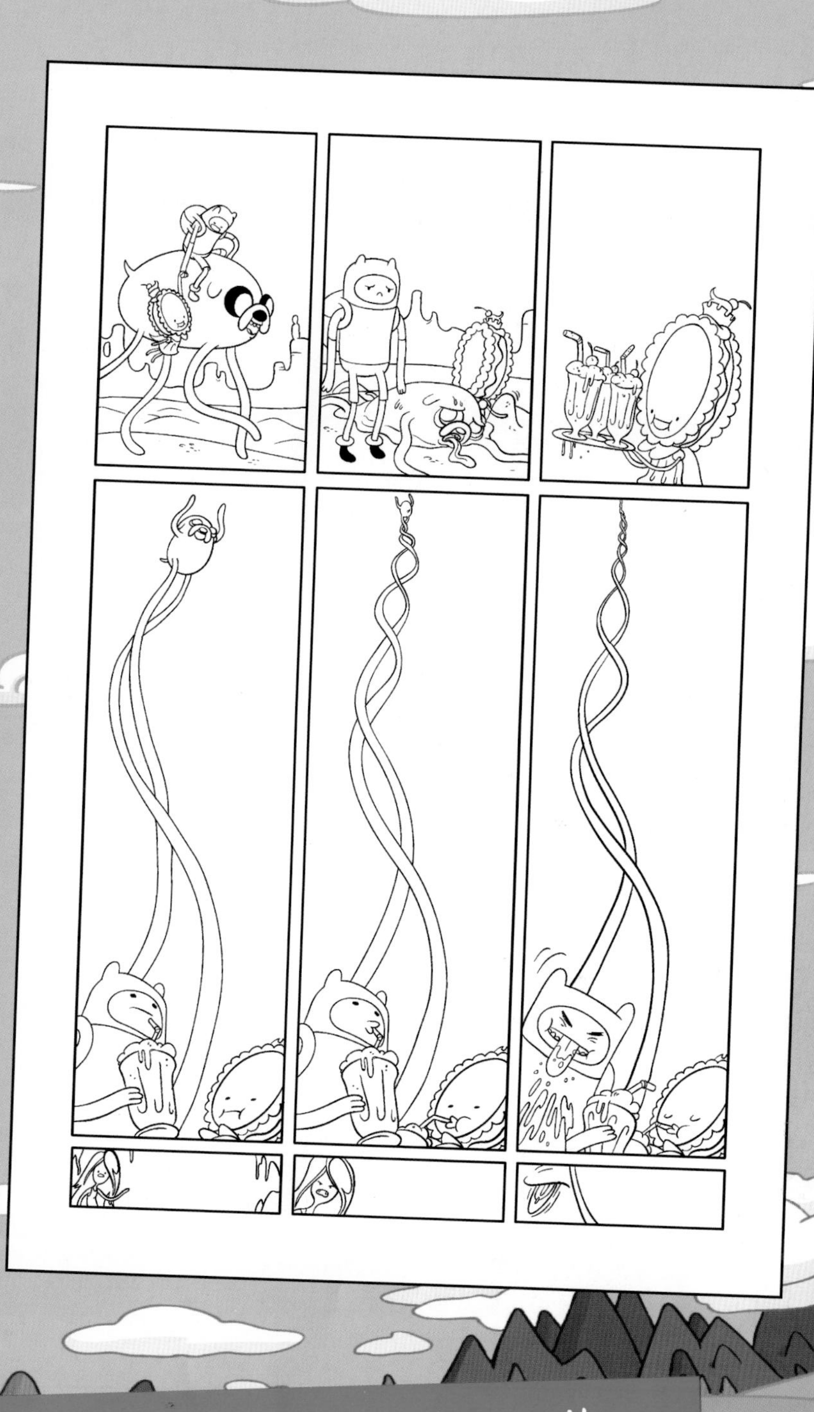

At this point I imagine writing this comic like a game of tennis: I send the ball over the net as hard as I can, confident that the other members of the team will be able to return it, and they do, but every single ball they hit returns as a hunk of solid gold.

DANG. TEAMWORK, YO.